*Just last week, very early,*
*tooth fairies fluttered high over the city.*

*No one looked up. No one saw the Underhills.*
*Esme pushed her glasses back on her nose.*
*"I just LOVE sleepovers at Grandma and Grandad's," she said.*
*"THERE THEY ARE!" shouted her big sister, April.*

*Ariel the dog's tail wagged and their wings*
*shivered in the wind as they*
*headed down.*

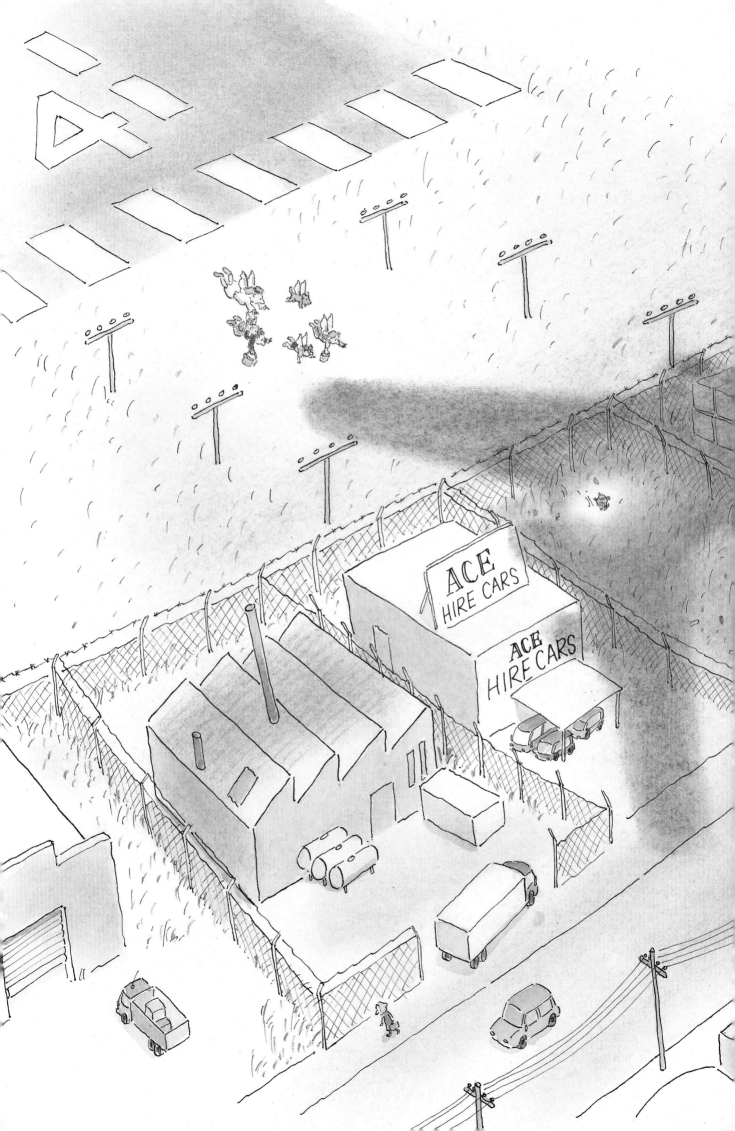

*For Silah*

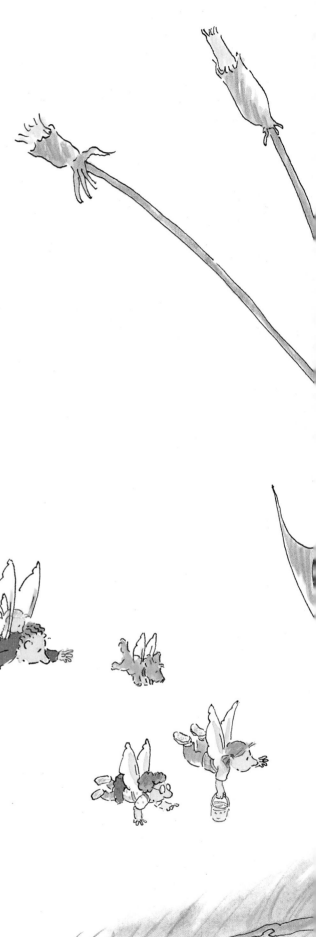

First published 2019 by Walker Books Ltd
87 Vauxhall Walk, London SE11 5HJ

10 9 8 7 6 5 4 3 2 1

© 2019 Blackbird Design Pty Ltd

The right of Bob Graham to be identified as author and illustrator
of this work has been asserted by him in accordance with the
Copyright, Designs and Patents Act 1988

This book has been typeset in Poliphilus and Blado MT

Printed in China

British Library Cataloguing in Publication Data:
a catalogue record for this book is available from the British Library

ISBN 978-1-4063-8761-2

www.walker.co.uk

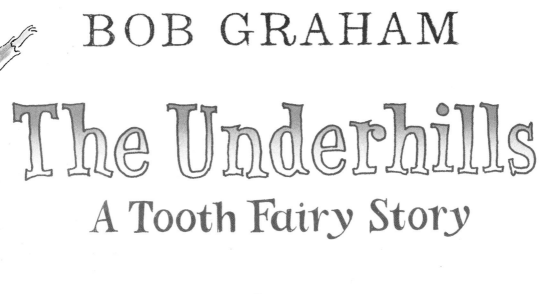

# BOB GRAHAM

# The Underhills

## A Tooth Fairy Story

WALKER BOOKS
AND SUBSIDIARIES
LONDON · BOSTON · SYDNEY · AUCKLAND

There were hugs. There were kisses.
"Mummy and Daddy have to work," said Esme.
Their new brother Vincent said nothing.
He couldn't talk yet.
"Urgent molar pickup on Main Street,"
Dad and Mum said together, and laughed.
Dad's arm around Mum made a soft crackle of wings.

April cleared her throat and stepped forward.
"Some tadpoles for you, Grandma," she said.
"Got them from the pond.
 Cute, aren't they?"

"Oh, thank you, April and Esme.
 And I see a lollipop stick floating on top."
"To sit on when they turn into frogs," said Esme.
"That's very thoughtful," replied Grandma.

"Vincent's mashed mulberries and nappies are
 in the bag, and treats for Ariel, too," called Mum.
"And our pyjamas," said Esme.
"And our books and toothbrushes," added April.

"Thanks for looking after them, Grandma and Grandad,"
shouted Mum and Dad. "We'll call or text. Must fly."
But their voices were drowned in sound.

Grandma and Grandad's!
A whole day and night.
Where the tea is always hot,
there's a bed of feathers for weary wings,
and pancakes with syrup for breakfast.

On each of their pillows, April and Esme
would find a chocolate waiting for them.
"Grandma things!" they called them.

And always special was the mixing of the fairy cakes …

and while they cooked, the tasting of the leftover chocolate.

And then there was Grandad,
working on the heavy bag
to keep in shape.

"Just whack it, Esme!" said Grandad. "Give it all you've got."
"I am, Grandad. I am!"
Then Grandma's phone rang.

"Who's that?
Oh! Hello, Fay
darling, I'll put
you on speaker."

Then Mum spoke. "A job just came in.
Small girl. Red coat. Arriving on
flight 417 from Ghana. Name of Akuba.
Baby tooth out. Somewhere in the pocket."

"Can WE do it, Mummy? Can WE get the tooth?"
There was a pause. "Well … be careful," said Mum.
"And remember," said Dad, "Akuba must never see you.
You are spirits of the air."

# "YESSS!!"

And there was a small flurry of airy excitement
in that teapot house by the airport fence.

Vincent's head was heavy with sleep,
so Grandad remained behind.

Grandad tied them together so that if he should fall asleep,
too, Vincent would not float off like a balloon.
Grandad settled down with his book,
*A Poem for Every Day of the Year.*

"Don't need your phones, kids," he said,
"there's a big chunk of life to see out there."
With still-warm cakes in Grandma's bag,
they flew over the fence.

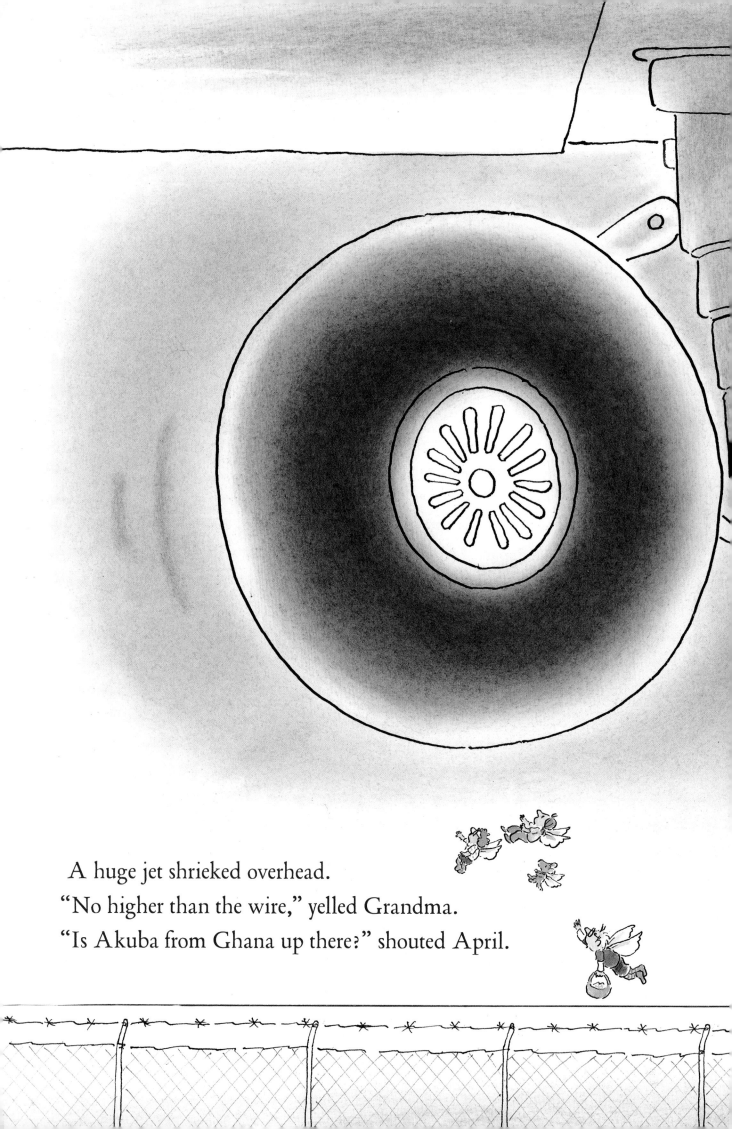

A huge jet shrieked overhead.

"No higher than the wire," yelled Grandma.

"Is Akuba from Ghana up there?" shouted April.

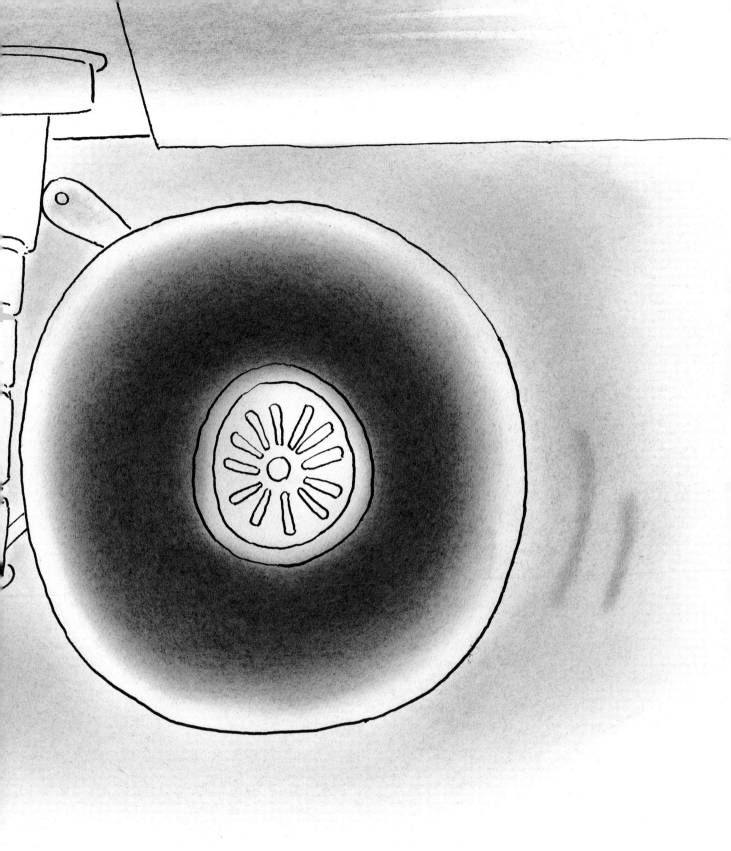

Grandma looked at her watch. "Not yet, but soon," she said.

"At the … the … terminable, Grandma?" said Esme.

"Yes, Esme, at the *terminal*."

"OH, GRANDMA!"
Down below in the terminal there was baggage,
noise, excitement and emotion overflowing.
And, up above, only the soft beating of wings.

"Can't see Akuba," said April, as the sisters bumped across the ceiling.

"In a little while she'll be here," said Grandma.

"Let's wait over there," said Esme,

"with the angels and the cupids."

"Brought your grandchildren today, Ophelia?" said the angel.

"Yes, this is April and this is Esme," replied Grandma.

"This is Beatrice, children. And this is Apollo and Mercury,
  the cupids."

"Pleased to meet you," said April and Esme.

"Shouldn't the cupids have bows and arrows, Grandma?"
 whispered April.
"They have to leave them at the door," said Grandma. "Security!"
"Would you like a fairy cake?" said Esme.
"Grandma made them."

"Are you waiting for Akuba, too?" Esme asked Mercury.
"Hmm! Nice cake. Who's Akuba?" he said.
"Little girl, red coat, baby tooth," said April.
"We don't do teeth," he said. "We cupids like to,
  well, just help people meet, I guess."

"And the angels?
They do the sad arrivals."

"And sometimes," Apollo added, "we just watch over."

"And the angels help to push the trolleys."

Then came the announcement:

**FLIGHT 417 FROM GHANA HAS LANDED!**

"IT'S AKUBA! IT'S AKUBA!"

And the Underhill sisters did cartwheels of excitement.

"Grandma, Grandma, we have no coin to give Akuba
for her tooth!" Grandma's hands flew to her face with shock.

"Oh, my dears! I forgot
to bring one," said Grandma.
"Wait! Check the drinks
machines down below."

And both the girls launched
themselves into the air.

They hovered in front of the vending machine,
their wings beating like small hummingbirds.

"I've FOUND one, April.
Help me!"

"And ... and ...
THERE SHE IS!"

"But where's the tooth, April?"
"Um, in her pocket, Esme?"
"Well, which pocket?" cried Esme.
"Try the right one," called April
  as they tumbled down,
    their fingers tight on the coin.

April grabbed for the pocket
and hung on gamely as Esme
swung from the coin with
her eyes shut tight.

And they crawled inside.

Deep inside the pocket,
April shouted, "HERE IT IS!"
"Shhh!" replied Esme.
"Oh, I think she heard us."
Akuba stopped and looked
all around.

"Quick, we have to leave," said April.
  And with the coin in Akuba's pocket, and April's arms around
  the tooth, Esme whispered in Akuba's ear,
"You heard nothing, Akuba. We are spirits of the air."
  As April and Esme returned to Grandma with the tooth,
  Akuba scratched her ear once and hurried to her mum.

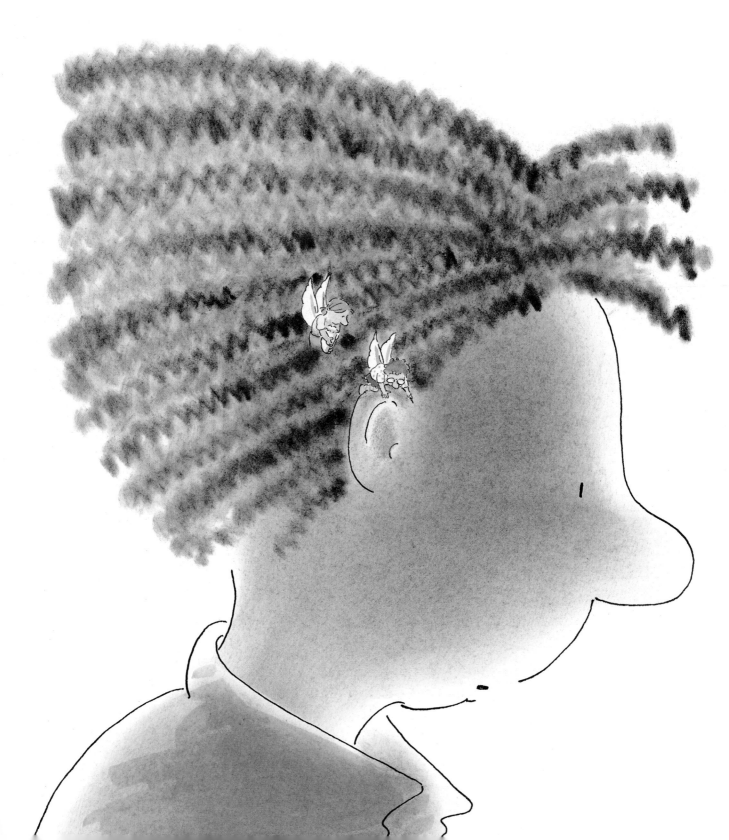

High up on the sign, Grandma was waiting.
"Grandma, Esme found a coin …"

"And we found Akuba," Esme continued.
"And the pocket," added April.

"And we found the tooth …"

"And left the coin …"
"And whispered in her ear …"
"And got out …"

"Just before they got in the taxi."

"OH!" said Grandma.

"Makes me nervous just thinking about it.
    Let's get you home."

Grandad was still reading from
*A Poem for Every Day of the Year,*
with Vincent's sweet breath in his ear.

He had read four months in one sitting.
"Don't this just beat it all," he said as Grandma,
the children and Ariel flew back over the fence.

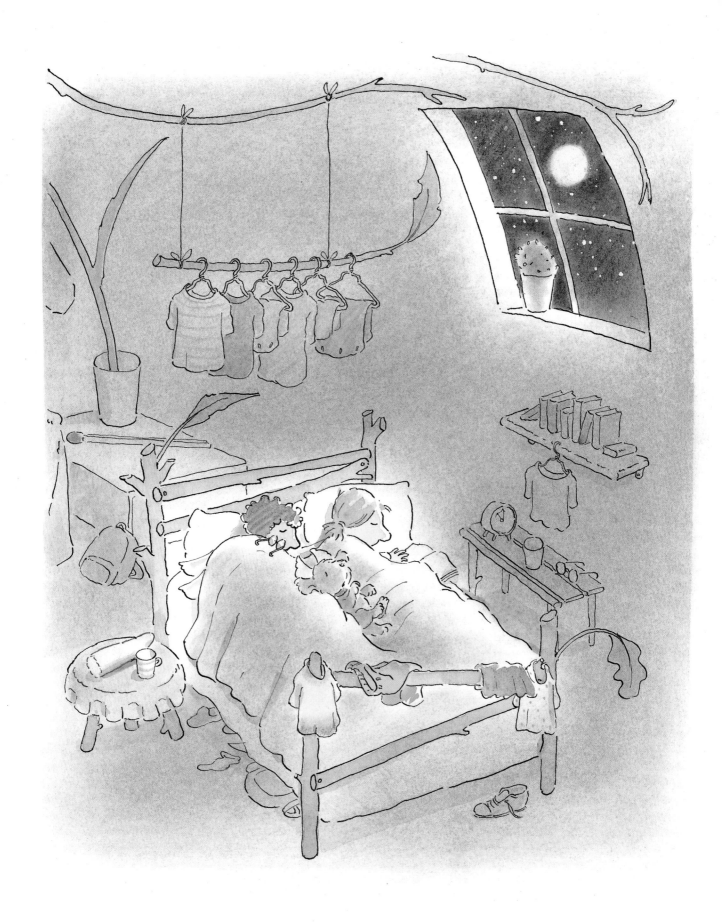

That night a full moon shone through the window of
the teapot home. April and Esme slept in a feather bed,
the baby tooth safe beside them.

Far across the city, the same moon shone on Akuba.
Her tooth now gone, a small coin she found in her
pocket now lay on her bedside table.
And she can't quite remember how it got there.

*The moon lay trapped for just a*
*moment in Grandma's gift.*
*The first tiny frog had come out of the water,*
*and the sound of its croak carried faintly up*
*over the silent airport and*
*out into the night.*